A Giant First-Start Reader

This easy reader contains only 36 different words,
repeated often to help the young reader develop
word recognition and interest in reading.

Basic word list for *Play Ball, Kate!*

a	her	play
and	here	plays
at	hit	puts
ball	is	she
bat	it	strike
cap	Kate	swing
catch	Kate's	takes
comes	of	team
coming	off	the
fast	on	this
glove	out	to
going	park	yea

Play Ball, Kate!

Written by Sharon Gordon

Illustrated by Don Page

Troll Associates

Library of Congress Cataloging in Publication Data

Gordon, Sharon.
   Play ball, Kate!

   Summary: Kate plays baseball with her team in the
park.
   [1. Baseball—Fiction]   I. Page, Don, 1946-
II. Title.
PZ7.G65936Pl   [E]   81-4855
ISBN 0-89375-525-7 (case)   AACR2
ISBN 0-89375-526-5 (pbk.)

Kate is going out to the park.

Kate takes her cap.

She takes her glove.

She takes her bat and ball.

Kate is going to play ball.

This is Kate's team.
Kate's team plays out at the park.

Yea team!

Kate puts on her cap.

She puts on her glove.

Play ball!

Here comes the ball.

The ball is coming fast.

Catch it, Kate!

Yea Kate! Yea team!

Kate takes off her cap.
She takes off her glove.

Kate takes her bat.

She takes a swing.

She takes a strike!

The ball is coming fast.

Kate takes a strike.

Here comes the fast ball.

Hit it, Kate!

She hit it!

Kate hit it *out of the park*!

Kate is coming fast.

Yea Kate! Yea team!